MW01173887

Tony Hawk

Pro Skateboarder

Marylou Morano Kjelle

P.O. Box 196
Hockessin, Delaware 19707
Visit us on the web: www.mitchelllane.com
Comments? email us: mitchelllane@mitchelllane.com

Printing   3   4   5   6   7   8   9

A Robbie Reader
Contemporary Biography/Science Biography

Albert Einstein	Albert Pujols	Alex Rodriguez
Aly and AJ	Amanda Bynes	Brittany Murphy
Charles Schulz	Dakota Fanning	Dale Earnhardt Jr. Donovan
McNabb	Drake Bell & Josh Peck	Dr. Seuss
Dylan & Cole Sprouse	Henry Ford	Hilary Duff
Jamie Lynn Spears	Jessie McCartney	Johnny Gruelle
LeBron James	Mandy Moore	Mia Hamm
Miley Cyrus	Philo T. Farnsworth	Raven Symone
Robert Goddard	Shaquille O'Neal	The Story of Harley-Davidson
Syd Hoff	Tiki Barber	Thomas Edison
Tony Hawk		

Library of Congress Cataloging-in-Publication Data
Kjelle, Marylou Morano.
    Tony Hawk / by Marylou Morano Kjelle.
         p. cm. — (A Robbie Reader)
    Includes bibliographical references and index.
      ISBN 1-58415-285-0 (library bound)
    1. Hawk, Tony—Juvenile literature. 2. Skateboarders—United States—Biography—
Juvenile literature. I. Title. II. Series.
GV859.813.H39K54 2005
796.22'092—dc22
                                    2004015442

ABOUT THE AUTHOR: Marylou Morano Kjelle is a freelance writer and photojournalist who lives and works in central New Jersey. She is a regular contributor to several local newspaper and online publications. Marylou writes a column for the *Westfield Leader/Times of Scotch Plains--Fanwood* called "Children's Book Nook," where she reviews children's books. She has written nine nonfiction books for young readers and has an M.S. degree in Science from Rutgers University.

PHOTO CREDITS: Cover—Getty Images; pp. 4, 18—Michael Cauldfield/WireImage.com; p. 6—Getty Images ; p. 7—Lee Celano/WireImage.com; pp. 8, 14, 27—Frazer Harrison/Getty Images; p. 10—Jed Jacobsohn/Getty Images; p. 12—Getty Images; p. 16—Ezra Shaw/Getty Images; p. 19—Lee Celano/WireImage.com; p. 20—Jaimie Trueblood/Getty Images; p. 22—Frank Micelotta/Getty Images; p. 24—Frederick M. Brown/Getty Images; p. 26—Arnaldo Magnani/Getty Images.

ACKNOWLEDGMENTS: The following story has been thoroughly researched and to the best of our knowledge represents a true story. While every possible effort has been made to ensure accuracy, the publisher will not assume liability for damages caused by inaccuracies in the data, and makes no warranty on the accuracy of the information contained herein. This story has not been authorized or endorsed by Tony Hawk.

PLB

TABLE OF CONTENTS

Tony is "upside down in the air" at a benefit carnival for children with AIDS in 2003.

A NEW RECORD

Tony Hawk had a goal. He wanted to do a very hard skateboard trick. It was called the 900. This stunt has two and a half midair spins and it must be done in less than a minute.

Tony had tried the 900 many times. He had been doing the trick since 1999, but not within the time allowed.

In 2003, Tony competed in the X Games in Los Angeles, California. It was time for the **Vert** Best Trick contest. Tony took his skateboard to the top of the ramp.

He skateboarded down one side of the ramp. He skateboarded up the other side. He tried the 900 and fell. Tony got back up and

Tony has worked hard to make skateboarding a popular sport.

Tony performs the 900 at the X Games in Los
Angeles, California, in 2003.

tried again. He kept trying until finally, on his
fourth try, he did it! And he did it in less than a
minute.

Tony had set a new record. He had been a
skateboard superstar before, but this stunt
would make him a legend. Many skateboarders
look up to Tony as their role model. Tony has
worked hard to make skateboarding as popular
as it is today.

Tony's mother, Nancy, is proud of Tony and the name he has made for himself by skateboarding.

BORN TO SKATE

Anthony Frank Hawk was born in San Diego, California, on May 12, 1968. His father, Frank, had been a navy pilot. He had flown bombers in World War II and in the Korean War. Tony's mother, Nancy, worked during the day and went to college at night.

Tony was the baby of the family. When he was born, his sisters, Lenore (LUH-nore) and Pat, were in college. His brother, Steve, was in eighth grade.

Nancy called Tony a "challenging" child. He needed a lot of attention. He had to have his own way. People said Tony was spoiled. His parents said he was loved.

Tony wraps up a competition at the X Games in California in 2000.

Tony was tough on himself. He had to be the best. He swam and played basketball and baseball. Whatever sport he played, he felt he had to win.

When Tony was six years old, his family moved to Tierrasanta (tee-ayr-uh-SAN-tah), San Diego. One day Steve gave Tony his old skateboard. Tony did not know what to do with it. "We goofed around on it," Tony said.

Tony liked to skateboard. Every day he went to Oasis (oh-AY-sis) Skatepark. For the first time, he was a happy kid.

Tony flies high above a ramp.

NATIONAL CHAMPION

Tony was skinny. His legs were so thin, he wore elbow pads on his knees. When he was on his skateboard, it was hard for him to build **momentum** (mo-MEN-tum). He had to make his slim body work for him.

Tony taught himself new tricks and stunts. His parents were his biggest fans. "They were my cheerleaders," he said.

Tony entered his first **competition** when he was 11 years old. He did not do well. He fell doing tricks he knew. Tony entered other contests. Sometimes he won. Sometimes he did not win.

Skateboarding became Tony's whole life. Other people were losing interest. Many skate

Former skateboarder Stacy Peralta asked Tony to join his team, the Bones Brigade, when Tony was 12.

parks closed. Frank wanted to keep the sport alive. In 1980 he helped start the California Amateur (AM-uh-chur) Skateboard League (CASL).

Dogtown is a company that makes skateboards. Dogtown made a deal with Tony. If Tony joined the Dogtown team, they would give Tony skateboards. Tony also had to **promote** Dogtown gear wherever he went. Tony took the deal.

When Tony was 12 years old, Stacy Peralta asked Tony to join his team. Stacy was a former skateboarder. His team was called the Bones Brigade (brig-AID). Now Tony would promote Stacy's company, called Powell-Peralta. Tony toured with the Bones Brigade. He entered many national competitions and won most of them.

Andy McDonald and Tony Hawk perform during the vert doubles competition at the 2000 X Games.

YOUNG PRO

In 1981, Tony's family moved to Cardiff, California. He went to San Dieguito High School. Tony got good grades, but he had no friends. Other students made fun of him because he was so tall (he would grow to be six feet four inches) and skinny. They called skateboarding a "loser" sport.

Tony switched to Torrey Pines High School. After school he would skate at Del Mar Surf and Turf Skatepark. He made friends with other skateboarders.

Tony turned **professional** when he was 14. He took third place in his first pro contest. His picture was on the cover of a skateboard magazine called *Thrasher*. He won his second pro competition at Del Mar.

CHAPTER FOUR

Tony's many skateboard tricks have made him a skateboard legend.

As a professional skateboarder, Tony entered many competitions. In 1992, he won a bronze medal in the skateboard Best Vert Trick Competition in Philadelphia.

Tony was always thinking up new skateboard tricks. He called them flippy tricks. When he was older, he would invent the Ollie 540 and the 720. The other skaters called him the Circus Skater and Birdman.

In 1983, his father, Frank, started the National Skateboard Association (NSA). The NSA formed the first pro **league**. Frank was president of the NSA. When Tony won the first NSA competition, people said Frank fixed the game so that his son would win. It was not true. Tony had won on his own, fair and square.

In 1999, Tony released his first skateboarding video game. In 2004, he hosted *Videogame Invasion*, a television show about video games. Here is Tony on the set of the show.

CHAPTER FIVE

BUSINESSMAN

Tony was 17 years old and a national champion. He won many competitions and made a lot of money. He bought a house and an expensive car. He had two skate ramps built in his yard.

Tony taught at a skateboard camp in Sweden. He made skateboarding movies and videos. But he never stopped trying to be a better skater. He did not forget about the 900. It was the only trick he could not do.

In 1990, people began to lose interest in skateboarding again. Tony needed a way to make money. In 1991, he started a skateboard company with some friends. He called it Birdhouse Projects.

Like father, like son. Tony's oldest son, Riley, also likes to skateboard.

By this time, Tony had married Cindy Dunbar. In 1992, their son, Hudson Riley, was born. They called him Riley.

The next few years were hard for Tony. Birdhouse Projects did not make money. Tony and Cindy got divorced. And Frank found out he had cancer.

Tony turned pro once more. In 1994, he entered a new set of games called the X Games. The *X* stands for "extreme." The X Games made skateboarding popular again. Birdhouse Projects took off. Things in Tony's life were looking up. Then, in 1995, Frank died. He did not see Tony land the 900.

In 1996, Tony married Erin Lee. They had two sons, Spencer (left) and Keegan (center, front).

SKATEBOARD LEGEND

By the time he **retired** in 1999, Tony Hawk had won 10 gold medals for skateboarding. Even though he no longer enters competitions, he is as busy as ever.

Tony and his second wife, Erin, have two young sons. Their names are Spencer and Keegan (KEE-gin). Tony coaches his oldest son, Riley, who also likes to skateboard. "I don't feel as old as other parents," said Tony.

Tony's skateboard company, Birdhouse Projects, has been doing very well. Tony also owns another company that makes children's skate clothing, called Hawk Clothing. He has video games, such as *Tony Hawk's Pro Skater* and *Tony Hawk's Underground,* that are very

Tony married Lhotse Merriam in January 2006.

popular. In 2006, he released *Tony Hawk's Downhill Jam* and *Tony Hawk's Project 8.*

Tony wants children to have a safe place to skate. He has set up the Tony Hawk Foundation to help build skate parks throughout the United States.

He also created the Tony Hawk Gigantic (jy-GAN-tik) Skatepark Tour for cable channel ESPN. The tours are almost as well known as the X Games. The Boom Boom HuckJam

Tony plays a video game with Dylan Sprouse (right) during the Playstation BANDtogether benefit while Alexis Waite (left) and Cole Sprouse watch.

extreme sports exhibitions are another Tony Hawk creation. These shows are given at Six Flags parks around the country. They feature BMXers, skateboarders, and Moto Xers.

In 2007, Six Flags gave Tony another honor: They opened the Tony Hawk Big Spin roller coasters in San Antonio and St. Louis. More were scheduled to be opened in other theme parks as well.

In 2004, Tony and Erin divorced. Two years later, he married Lhotse Merriam. They live in San Diego, near where Tony grew up.

Tony isn't just a famous face. He's worked hard at being everything that he is. He's a father. He's a businessman. He's a national champion. But most of all, he is a skateboard legend.

1968   Tony Hawk is born on May 12.

1976   Brother Steve gives Tony his old skateboard, a blue Bahne banana board.

1981   Tony joins Bones Brigade.

1982   Tony turns pro.

1983   Tony's father, Frank, starts National Skateboarding Association.

1990   Tony marries Cindy Dunbar.

1992   Tony and Cindy's son Riley is born. Tony starts Birdhouse Projects.

1994   Tony and Cindy divorce.

1995   Tony competes in the first X Games. His father dies of cancer.

1996   Tony marries Erin Lee.

1999   Tony and Erin's son Spencer is born. With Activision, Tony creates *Tony Hawk's Pro Skater* video game for PlayStation. Tony lands his first 900, but not within time allowed. He retires from competition, though he still skateboards every day.

2000   *Tony Hawk's Pro Skater 2* is released and jumps to number one.

2001   Tony's third son, Keegan, is born.

2002   Tony Hawk Charitable Foundation is established to help build skateparks around the country. He launches Boom Boom HuckJam, an extreme sports exhibition.

2003   Tony makes skateboarding history by completing the first 900 within 45 seconds.

2004   Tony and Erin divorce.

2006   Tony marries Lhotse Merriam in January.

2007   Tony Hawk's Big Spin Roller Coaster opens at Six Flags St. Louis and San Antonio.

Tony Hawk has appeared in the following films and videos,
plus many others:

1984 *Bones Brigade Video Show*
1985 *Bones Brigade 2: Future Primitive*
1986 *Thrashin'*
1987 *Police Academy 4: Citizens on Patrol*
1989 *Bones 4: Public Domain*
1989 *Gleaming the Cube*
2000 *The End*
2000 *Tony Hawk's Trick Tips Vol. 1: Skateboard Basics*
2001 *Dogtown and Z-Boys*
2001 *CKY3*
2002 *Ultimate X: The Movie*
2003 *Haggard: The Movie*
2003 *Over the Edge: Boards X*
2004 *Tony Hawk's Secret Skatepark Tour*

Tony Hawk Video Games
1999 *Tony Hawk's Pro Skater*
2000 *Tony Hawk's Pro Skater 2*
2001 *Tony Hawk's Pro Skater 3*
2002 *Tony Hawk's Pro Skater 4*
2003 *Tony Hawk's Underground*
2004 *Tony Hawk's Underground 2*
2005 *Tony Hawk's American Wasteland*
     Tony Hawk's American SK8land
2006 *Tony Hawk's Project 8*
     Tony Hawk's Downhill Jam

competition (com-peh-TIH-shun)—a contest.

league (LEEG)—a group of teams that compete against each other.

momentum (mo-MEN-tum)—speed.

professional (pro-FEH-shun-al)—someone who is trained and is an expert in his or her field.

promote (pruh-MOTE)—to talk about something in order to makes sales.

retired (rih-TIRED)—to stop working professionally

vert—short for *vertical;* skateboard tricks done on a ramp that is nearly straight up and down.

FIND OUT MORE

Books

Braun, Eric. *Tony Hawk.* Minneapolis: Lerner Publications Company, 2004.

Christopher, Matt. *On the Halfpipe with Tony Hawk.* New York: Little Brown, 2001.

Powell, Ben. *Skateboarding.* Minneapolis: Lerner Publications Company, 2004.

Stewart, Mark. *One Wild Ride: The Life of Skateboarding Superstar Tony Hawk.* Brookfield, Conn.: Millbrook Press, 2001.

Web Addresses

Tony Hawk's Official Fan Site
http://www.tonyhawk.com

Tony Hawk's Boom Boom Huck Jam
http://www.boomboomhuckjam.com

"Tony Hawk Writes Skateboarding History with 900 in Best Trick at X Games," by Steve McDonald
http://skateboardlink.com/comps/99xgames/tony900.htm

X Games Website
http://expn.go.com